# Mystery
## in the Wings

### Carolyn Crimi
#### Illustrated by Susan Gal

Rigby

# Contents

# Chapter 1

# A Star Is Born!

Kit Conroy hopped on her scooter and soared down the street. She got the part! She got the part! Now her summer would be saved! Instead of going to the boring public pool every day, she would be rehearsing. She was so excited about telling her friend Spencer about her part in the play, she could hardly stand it. Kit knew he would be happy for her. He was, after all, the one who was always telling her she was so dramatic.

The roles were posted on the bulletin board at the Gloria Canterbury Theater. Her mom had told her the parts would be announced that afternoon, so Kit hurried after lunch to check the bulletin board. Sure enough, her name was there—next to the part of the Mad Hatter, the part she wanted.

On the way home from the theater, Kit sang the old show tune "Hooray for Hollywood!" at the top of her lungs. People stared, but she didn't care. She got the part! She got the part!

Gliding to a stop, Kit jumped off her scooter,

folded it up, and carried it to its spot behind the front bushes. Once inside the Conroy's brick house, she flung her backpack, her helmet, and her protective pads in the front hall and raced up the stairs to her bedroom. Her computer was on and waiting for her in the corner of her room. She logged on with a few quick keystrokes.

Mooch wandered in and stood by her desk, staring at her with his "please feed me" look.

"No, I don't have any food for you," Kit said without looking down at him.

Mooch grunted in defeat and curled up under her desk. She reached down and patted the old bulldog's head.

"Sorry, Mooch, dinner's not for another two hours," Kit said.

She sighed when she saw her empty mailbox. Spencer hadn't e-mailed her in three days.

She knew he was probably busy getting used to his new neighborhood, but it still bugged her that he hadn't found time to write one e-mail.

Dear Spencer,
OK, why haven't you written me?
How busy could you be, anyway? And—

Before she could finish her sentence, the Instant Message window blinked on.

**Segreti410:** Hey.

**StarGirl:** Well, it's about time.

**Segreti410:** I've only been here three days. I haven't even unpacked yet.

**StarGirl:** I doubt that. Knowing you, your room is probably all set up by now.

Kit pictured her best friend sitting at his tidy desk, his wild hair sticking out from under his cap.

She knew he was unpacked and that his room was in perfect order. But she also knew that he liked to pretend as though he was just like most messy kids, which was why he was lying about not being unpacked. Except for his crazy mop of hair, he was the tidiest kid she knew, but he tried to keep that a secret. Spencer knew that being neat was not cool for a kid his age.

**StarGirl:** Guess what?

**Segreti410:** Mooch decided to run away to the circus?

**StarGirl:** Try again.

**Segreti410:** Umm, YOU decided to run away to the circus?

**StarGirl:** Will you be serious?!

**Segreti410:** OK, OK, don't have a meltdown. What's up?

**StarGirl:** I got a part in the summer play!

**Segreti410:** You did? Cool. Way cool. When do rehearsals start?

Mooch nudged Kit with his flattened nose. Kit pushed him away gently. Downstairs she could hear her mom putting groceries away.

"Kit, are you here? I could use some help," Mom called.

"I'm online!" Kit called to her mom. "I'll be down in a second!"

> **StarGirl:** Oops. Gotta go. Mom's here and she needs help with the groceries. But here's the news in a nanosecond: the play is "Alice in Wonderland," which is only my favorite book of all time. I got the role I wanted, the Mad Hatter, and my MOM is going to direct it. I'm the youngest one in the whole cast, which is kind of ick, but the other people seem OK. I hope.
>
> **Segreti410:** The Mad Hatter? Sounds like the perfect part for you. Fill me in when you have more time.
>
> **StarGirl:** OK!
>
> **Segreti410:** Bye.
>
> **StarGirl:** Bye.

Kit logged off and headed downstairs with Mooch at her heels.

Mom was putting away a quart of skim milk when Kit bounded into the kitchen. "Hey there," she said.

Kit gave her mom a hug. "Thanks so much for giving me the role of the Mad Hatter. It's a great part."

Mom pushed Kit's bangs back from her face and planted a kiss on her forehead. "Well, you deserved it. You did a great job in the audition. I just don't want you to think I was playing favorites. You were the best one for the part. I mean that," Mom said firmly.

"I hope so. I'm kind of nervous, being the youngest one in the cast and all," said Kit. She picked up one of Mooch's treats without her mom noticing it and slipped the treat into Mom's pocket.

"You'll do just great. I know you will," said Mom.

Mooch whined and nudged Mom with his nose. "Oh, Mooch, what are we going to do with you?" asked Mom.

"Why don't you give him a treat? You've got one in your pocket," Kit said.

A frown passed over Mom's face. She reached into the pocket of her overalls and then smiled.

"You've done it again. You're really something, you know that?" Mom said, feeding Mooch his treat.

Kit's family had played this game ever since she was a little girl. It started in second grade when Kit changed schools after the family moved to New York from California. Kit was nervous about her first day, so Kit's father wrote out her favorite knock-knock joke on a tiny piece of paper and stuck it into her pocket without her knowing it. Every day after that, he wrote Kit little notes and stuck them in her pocket or her backpack. Sometimes he would give her a quarter or a tiny toy. Kit started doing it, too, and before long the whole family was slipping little notes and gifts into each other's pockets and backpacks and briefcases. Kit had gotten really good at it and was able to sneak just about anything into anyone's pocket.

"Does Dad know I got the part?" asked Kit, stashing two pints of fat-free ice cream in the freezer.

"I haven't had time to call him yet. I've been so busy with everything—casting, programs, you name it. Why don't you call him? I know he'd love to hear the news directly from you. He's probably out on the shoot now, but you can call him later tonight."

As an advertising executive, Kit's dad was always on the road shooting commercials. He would be gone for the next two weeks this time. He was shooting a commercial for a dishwashing detergent called SoapEeze. He was going to try to show real animals washing dishes with SoapEeze. His commercials were always funny, just like him.

"Have they found a dog or a cat that can wash dishes yet?" asked Kit.

Mom shook her head, chuckling. "Nope." She put away the last can of soup. "Hey, how about pizza for dinner? I really don't feel like cooking."

"Hmm, sounds suspiciously unhealthy. Are you sure you can risk it?" Kit asked, grinning. Mom was always trying to eat healthy, low-fat foods.

"For your information, pizza is a very nutritional

food," Mom said. "It has calcium, vitamin A, vitamin C, and, um, all kinds of other things you should be eating. Besides, it tastes good."

"And the two billion calories?" Kit asked.

"I'll worry about that tomorrow," Mom replied.

Kit never could figure out what her mom was worried about. At forty-four, Kit thought she was the prettiest mom in town. Years of being an actress on a television sitcom made people notice her wherever she went, so she always tried to eat well and exercise to stay in shape.

"Uh-oh!" said Mom, peering out the kitchen window. "There's Leslie. Looks like she's coming over. I wonder if she's heard the news."

Kit looked over Mom's shoulder and saw Mrs. Pierce tromping through their yard to the back door.

The doorbell rang. Mom inhaled sharply and swung the door open.

"Leslie! Hi! How are you?" said Mom, a little too cheerfully, Kit thought.

"Hello, Pamela," said Mrs. Pierce.

Mrs. Pierce's large, dark eyes had purplish smudges under them and her mouth turned down at the corners. Kit couldn't remember ever hearing Mrs. Pierce laugh.

"I heard the news that you'll be directing 'Alice in

Wonderland.' I thought I'd come by and congratulate you," she said, frowning.

"Why thanks, Leslie. That's sweet of you," said Mom.

Mrs. Pierce snorted. "I think that's the first time someone has ever called me 'sweet,'" she said.

"Well, I mean it," said Mom. "I think it's very nice that you came by. Would you like some coffee or tea?"

Mrs. Pierce shook her head. "I have to be going soon. I just wanted to wish you luck. You're certainly going to need it."

"Oh?" Mom said. She shifted from one foot to the other. "What makes you say that?"

"Well, look at that cast you have. Erika is so spoiled. She'll never listen to what you have to say. And who did I see on your stage crew? Randy? He has such an attitude problem. And Kit . . ." she looked quickly over to Kit and then looked away. "I'm sure she'll be just fine, but she's new to theater and quite young. It might be very difficult for her."

Kit felt like she had been slapped across the cheek. New to theater? Her?

Mom folded her arms across her chest and pursed her lips. "Kit has plenty of theater experience, Leslie," she said curtly. "In fact, Kit has more experience than most of the cast. She used to come to the studio and watch me rehearse when we lived in California." She curled her arm around Kit and drew her closer. "And Erika is a perfectly sweet girl. Randy has had some problems in the past, but they're over now. I know he's ready to move on." Mom stood up straighter and looked Mrs. Pierce directly in the eyes.

Mrs. Pierce glanced at her watch. "Well, I'm running late. I hope you don't think I was being too harsh. I'm sure everything will be fine. But I was curious—will you need someone to help with the costumes? I'd be happy to. Really."

Mrs. Pierce was a whiz with a sewing machine. Everyone knew it. Kit held her breath, waiting to hear what Mom's response was.

Mom smiled a little too broadly. "That would be great. Thanks for offering. I can't wait to talk to you about it."

"Good," Mrs. Pierce said. "It's a deal." She waved her hand at Mom. "See you later."

After she left, Kit turned to Mom. "You're going to have *her* do the costumes? Are you kidding?"

Mom sighed and grinned. "Leslie has . . . problems. But she's a wonderful seamstress."

"Yeah, but Mom, she was so, so . . ."

"Infuriating? I know she can be difficult. But she's always had a hard time with other people's success. I'm sure it really bothers her that the committee asked me to direct this play after she's been with the theater for so long. Maybe letting her do the costumes will help her realize we appreciate her other talents."

Mom could be annoyingly nice at times, but Kit admired her for it. There was no way *she'd* ever let Mrs. Pierce do the costumes after what she said about her lack of theater experience. She might have only had roles in school plays, but she definitely had experience. The whole conversation made Kit furious.

"If I were you, I wouldn't trust her, Mom," said Kit.

Mom barked out a laugh. "Don't be silly. She's harmless." She clapped her hands together. "So, what do you want on your pizza? Anchovies? Sardines? Pickled eggs?"

"Very funny," said Kit. "Just the usual, please."

"Coming right up," said Mom.

Later, when they were at the kitchen table with the gooey cheese pizza between them, Kit thought again about Mrs. Pierce and what she had said. Why does she want to make the costumes if she thinks the show will be a disaster?

Strange, very strange.

# Chapter 2

# First Day of
# Rehearsal

Kit coasted to a stop in front of the theater. She gave Mooch a quick pat on his big head and slipped him a treat for keeping up with her.

"Sure does look busy in there, Moochie," she said to him, folding up her scooter. She took off her helmet and pads and stuffed them into her backpack.

Two men wearing faded T-shirts and work boots hauled a ladder through the front door while a woman wearing overalls carried a cardboard box marked "memorabilia" up the stone steps.

A month ago the mayor decided to change the Edgeview Community Theater into the Gloria Canterbury Theater. Kit thought it was a pretty goofy idea, since most people had no idea who Gloria Canterbury was. At least not kids her age. But some of the older people in town remembered her from her famous role in some dusty old black-and-white movie that Kit could never watch without falling asleep.

Gloria also won some awards for Broadway plays. Kit's mom thought she was a "miracle onstage." Kit thought she was a total yawner.

After Gloria died last winter, the town decided she should be honored, since she started her stage career right there at the Edgeview Theater. They changed the name of the theater to the Gloria Canterbury Theater and asked Gloria Canterbury's niece, Mrs. Greer, to help display some of the great actress' memorabilia, which she left to the theater in her will. Kit was sure it would be a bunch of boring stuff like dried-up rose bouquets or old, yellowed gloves.

"C'mon, Moochie," she said.

Mooch grunted as he climbed each step of the theater. He was always grunting, ever since he was a puppy. It usually made Kit giggle, but not today. The first day of rehearsal was always nerve-racking.

Walking through the front door, Kit bumped into an older woman wearing a bright red suit.

"Oops, I'm sorry," Kit said.

The woman smiled at her. "Not your fault," she replied breezily. "And who's this?" she asked, bending down to pat Mooch.

"That's Mooch. He eats," said Kit.

"Sounds like a good profession to me," said the woman.

13

The woman wearing overalls approached them. "Excuse me, Mrs. Greer, but where would you like the silver compact?" she asked.

Mrs. Greer, Kit remembered, was Gloria Canterbury's niece. Kit backed away, suddenly feeling very shy.

"Hmm," said Mrs. Greer. "I'll have to look at the display one more time. Will you excuse me?" she asked Kit.

"Yeah, sure," Kit mumbled. She could feel her freckles burning up on her red face.

The glass case in the lobby of the building was open. The woman wearing overalls spoke very animatedly to Mrs. Greer as the two of them peered into the case.

Kit snuck up behind them with Mooch at her side. Spencer was always saying she was a snoop. She kept telling him that great actresses should always be watching other people very closely. It helps them with their craft.

The case had exactly the kinds of things Kit thought it would have in it. A gleaming silver compact sat between a pair of long white gloves and a silver brush and comb set. The compact was a fancy, old-fashioned round case—the type that ladies kept face powder in. A couple of tarnished acting awards were lined up on the right-hand side. A few autographed black-and-white photographs of Gloria Canterbury stood behind all the items.

Boring, boring, boring. Kit couldn't see what the big fuss was.

"I think the doll should be prominently displayed, don't you, Mrs. Greer? I mean the compact is quite nice, but I don't think it's as important as the doll."

Mrs. Greer nodded. "Perhaps you're right. I guess I just never did like dolls."

The woman in overalls bent down and picked up a doll from the box marked "memorabilia." It was a little bigger than the average fashion doll, and it looked like it was made of china instead of plastic. The doll wore a shimmering white gown, shoulder-length blonde hair, and dark glasses. It practically oozed glamour.

"Wow," Kit whispered.

The two women turned around. Kit could feel her face burning up again.

"I'm sorry. I was just, well, I don't know . . ." Kit stammered.

Mrs. Greer smiled. "Would you like to hold the doll?" she asked.

Kit wasn't wild about dolls, but there was something about this doll that screamed for Kit's attention. It had, well, an attitude. That was the only way Kit could describe it.

"Are you sure that's a good idea, Mrs. Greer?" asked the woman in overalls.

"Of course. Dolls are made for little girls," she said.

Mrs. Greer took the doll from the other woman and handed it to Kit.

"I really don't like dolls," said Kit, "but this one is different. She looks like she owns the world."

"The real Gloria Canterbury *did* own the world," said Mrs. Greer.

Her voice had changed, Kit noticed. Was it sadness Kit heard, or something else?

"That doll is an exact likeness of her," Mrs. Greer continued in the same breezy tone as before. "The dolls came out right after she starred in the movie 'Midnight.' This is a replica of the dress she wore in the film." Mrs. Greer ran her pale, dry fingers over the satiny dress. "There were only 50 of these dolls made. The war came and production stopped. That's why this one is so expensive."

Kit swallowed hard. "Um, how much is it worth?" she asked, her hands shaking slightly.

"Oh, about $50,000," said Mrs. Greer.

Kit gasped and handed the doll back.

Mrs. Greer chuckled. "Don't worry, it's insured!" she said. She fit the doll into a wire stand and propped her up in the middle of the case.

Erika Standler, the teenage girl who was playing the role of Alice, rushed into the building, tying back her long blonde hair with a ribbon. She stopped in her tracks when she saw the Gloria Canterbury doll.

"That is the most beautiful doll I've ever seen!" she cried.

17

"You think so?" asked Mrs. Greer.

"Definitely," said Erika. "I have a doll collection at home. I have 63 dolls from all over the world, but I've never seen anything like that!"

"It's a very rare doll," explained Mrs. Greer.

"I'll say," said Erika. She stared at the doll the way Mooch stared at pork chops. "I wish it were mine," she said softly. She flicked her long blonde ponytail over her shoulder. "Well, I better get to rehearsal." She eyed Kit. "You too," she said, strutting into the theater.

Kit was about to tell her that she had arrived there way before Erika, but then she heard her mother's strained voice behind her.

"Where have you been?" Mom asked. "I've been looking all over for you."

Kit turned and saw her mother walking toward her.

Mooch woofed. Mom groaned. "Oh, Kit, why did you bring Mooch with you?"

"He won't do anything wrong," said Kit. "You know how lazy he is."

A voice called from inside the theater. "Pamela, we need you in here."

Mom rolled her eyes. "We'll talk about Mooch later," she said, hurrying back into the theater.

Kit knew her mom was extra nervous about being asked to direct this play. It would be the first play in the newly remodeled theater.

The woman wearing overalls checked her watch, then called the two men over. "Unfortunately, we need to get going, Mrs. Greer," she said.

"Oh, don't you worry. I'll take care of the items in the display case. You all run along."

The woman in overalls left with the two men who had carried in the trunk.

"That's a very cool doll," Kit said to Mrs. Greer.

"Thanks. I think so, too," she said, smoothing the doll's dress.

Kit stashed her backpack and her scooter in the corner of the lobby. She tugged lightly on Mooch's leash and led him toward the doorway of the theater.

The first person Kit spotted when she peered into the theater was a shy young man with stringy hair and bad posture. He was talking to Mom. The boy looked familiar to her. She remembered him coming over to their house once. His name was Randy Stickle. He must be the Randy Mrs. Pierce was talking about. Mom had invited him over to dinner after he got into some trouble at the high school. His grades had started going down. His teachers said that he didn't pay attention in school. But in spite of his problems,

Randy had graduated and now lived in a tiny apartment in town. Mom was worried about him, though. And since she always rooted for the underdog, she gave him a job as a stagehand.

"If someone doesn't give that kid a break, he'll get into trouble," Mom said. "I just know it."

Mom worried about everyone. It was a wonder she had any time leftover to worry about Kit.

"Kit, come on. Leslie needs to fit you for your costume," Mom said, motioning Kit into the theater.

Kit suddenly felt like she was about five years old. Everywhere she looked, grown-ups were busy with something—props, lighting, costumes. The air seemed charged with nervous energy, most of it coming from Mom.

Mrs. Pierce was standing on stage with a tape measure around her neck. Kit unhooked Mooch's leash and led him to the center of the aisle where she could watch him.

"Stay," she ordered him.

Mooch collapsed on the floor with a heavy sigh. In just a few seconds Kit knew he would be snoring.

Kit climbed the steps along the side of the stage to where Mrs. Pierce stood waiting for her. Kit noted that she was frowning, and seemed impatient.

Mrs. Pierce looked down at her clipboard. "Now,

what part do you have again?" she asked.

Kit cleared her throat. "The Mad Hatter."

"That's right. All right, let me take some measurements." Mrs. Pierce whipped her tape measure from around her neck and started measuring Kit like an old pro. Within minutes she had all the information she needed.

"There, all done," she said briskly.

"Wow, that was fast," said Kit.

"I've been in theater for a long, long time, Kit."

One of the stagehands popped her head out from behind the curtains. "Mrs. Pierce, you have a phone call in the office," she said.

Mrs. Pierce shook her head. "Who could be calling me here?" she asked and walked off the stage in a huff.

"OK," Mom said in her loud director's voice. "Let's do a quick read-through of the first act. Everyone on stage, please."

The actors and actresses climbed up the steps. Morry Cheever, the man who would be playing the White Rabbit, had white hair and half-glasses. To Kit, he looked just like the White Rabbit. The Queen of Hearts would be played by Sophie Gentry, a round woman with a tiny, round mouth. Holly Mackes, who was just a few years older than Kit, was the March

Hare. Jeff Crafft, one of Kit's neighbors, would be the Cheshire Cat. He had a mischievous grin that made him perfect for the part. A few other actors whom Kit didn't know tromped up the steps and waited for directions.

As everyone settled in, Kit overheard Jeff and Sophie talking about Randy.

"Why would Pamela ask *him* to be a stagehand?" Jeff asked.

"He's nothing but trouble," said Sophie. "I heard he was nearly suspended from high school, although I'm not sure what for."

"And he's always scowling," said Jeff. "He has a huge chip on his shoulder, that's for sure."

Kit suddenly felt sorry for Randy. Mom had told her that none of the stories about Randy were true. People just liked to pick on him for some reason. In a small town like Edgeview, that could really make things hard for the person being picked on.

"Where's Erika?" asked Mom.

Heads swiveled around.

"She just left for a second," said Holly. "Something about brushing her teeth. She has a thing about brushing her teeth," Holly added. She shrugged when everyone stared at her quizzically. "I don't know. Ask *her* about it. I just know that in every play we've been in so far, she's always brushing her teeth or her hair."

A few people giggled. Mom frowned slightly and clapped her hands.

"OK, we'll have to start without her. But that light—it's so bright. Randy? Can you soften that light a little?" Mom waited for Randy's response, but there was none.

"Where *is* everybody?" Mom asked, rubbing her temples with her fingers.

"Who knows where he is," Jeff whispered to Sophie.

"Probably getting into trouble somewhere," Sophie added.

Poor Randy. Those two were not going to let up on him. Kit could feel her cheeks flush with anger. She had to say something to them!

"You know . . ." she started.

Her speech was cut off by a loud scream that came from offstage.

# Chapter 3

# The Missing Necklace

Kit looked around quickly.

"Where did that come from?" asked Mom.

"I think it came from backstage," said Kit.

"Definitely," added Jeff. "I'll go check it out."

Mom followed Jeff. Kit followed a few steps behind her.

Mom spun around and faced Kit. "Where do you think you're going?" she asked.

"I'm going to see what happened," Kit said.

"Oh no, you're not," said Mom. "Leave this up to Jeff and me, OK?"

It was not OK, but before Kit had a chance to argue, Erika rushed onstage from behind the curtain.

"It's gone!" she yelled, storming up to Mom. "Someone has taken it!" Erika's face was bright red.

"Calm down," said Mom. She reached out for Erika, but Erika pulled away. "What's gone?" Mom asked.

Erika let out an exasperated breath of air. "My lucky four-leaf-clover pendant," she explained impatiently. "It kept coming unclasped, so I took it off and put it in my purse. Now it's not there! Someone took it!"

Mom paused, then asked, "Was that you who just screamed?"

Erika shook her head in disbelief. "Of course that was me! That pendant is the most important thing I own! I've never performed without it! I've never even rehearsed without it! We've got to find the thief right now!"

And Spencer said *Kit* was dramatic? Erika was acting like some silly soap opera star.

"Maybe it fell off and you just forgot," said Kit.

Erika glared at her. "No," she said coolly, "I remember taking it off. I'm not an idiot."

"No one is saying you're an idiot," said Mom. She shot Kit a warning glance. "I think what Kit means is that with all the excitement of the first day of rehearsals, maybe it fell off and you didn't realize it."

Erika stuck her chin out. "Well, you're wrong," she said. "Someone took it, and I bet I know who did!"

Everyone looked at Erika, waiting for her to speak. She paused for effect. It was obvious to Kit that Erika loved this attention.

"Well, it had to be Randy, of course," Erika said finally.

"Randy?" Kit exclaimed. "Why would Randy want a necklace?"

Erika flicked her blonde ponytail off of her shoulder. "It's sterling silver," she informed Kit, "and it's inlaid with real green enamel. I saw him eyeing it before. He had to have taken it."

"That's the dumbest thing I ever heard," said Kit.

"Kit," Mom warned, shooting her a "be quiet if you know what's good for you" look. "Erika, why don't we all look around for it? Perhaps it dropped out of your purse."

"You can look all you want, but you won't find it," Erika said. She plunked down on a chair in the middle of the stage.

"Oh brother," Kit said under her breath. Holly snickered. Mom shot Kit another killer look.

Mom clapped her hands again, director style. "OK, everyone, let's look around for Erika's necklace."

"Where did you see it last?" asked Sophie.

"I told you, I took it off and put it in my purse," Erika snapped.

"Erika, we're only trying to help," Mom said.

"It would 'help' if you got Randy up here and asked him about my necklace," Erika said.

Mom rubbed her temples again. "I can see you're upset, Erika, but accusing Randy is a very serious thing, and I'm not comfortable with it."

"Where is Randy, anyway?" Sophie asked. "He's been gone for a while."

Some of the cast members murmured. Sophie and Jeff looked at each other knowingly. Kit knew what they were thinking by the smug expressions on their faces.

Suddenly Kit wanted to find Randy very, very badly. She could care less about the necklace, but if Randy didn't defend himself soon she knew he'd be in trouble with the cast. Everyone thought he did it. Kit had to prove them wrong.

"I'll go look for him," Kit said.

Mom looked at her, then shrugged. "OK, Kit. The rest of you, keep looking for Erika's necklace. It might be around here somewhere."

Kit scurried down the stage steps. She looked for Mooch, but saw he was gone. He must have gone hunting for treats somewhere, and was probably nosing his way through her backpack at that very moment. He was a lazy dog, except when it came to food. Her first priority, though, was to find Randy. She knew Mooch wouldn't go far without her at his side.

Kit decided to check in the basement first, where

the prop room and the costume room were. One of Randy's jobs was finding the right props for the play and finding new ones if needed.

Kit had been in the theater's basement a few times before when her mom was in plays, and each time she found it really spooky. Kit crept down the narrow, creaky steps. When she got to the bottom, she paused and looked around. Piles of junk were stacked up everywhere. It was cold and damp and smelled like moldy old rags. Dimly lit hallways turned this way and that, like a maze, leading to weird little nooks and crannies and closets. A person could get lost down there in a second.

A cold draft whispered past. Kit shuddered. It felt like there was an open door somewhere. It was probably the door to the outside. Maybe Randy left the building to get something from his car.

"Randy?" Kit called. "Are you down here?"

Was that a footstep? Kit couldn't tell. But she could sort of *feel* someone down there with her.

"Hello?" Kit called again. "Who's down here?"

Now Kit was sure she heard footsteps. Whoever it was wasn't answering her. And the footsteps were getting closer.

"OK, you can stop playing around now," Kit said, her voice quivering. "Randy, is that you?"

A door to Kit's left creaked open suddenly. Kit gasped and jumped back. Her muscles tensed, waiting for the person to emerge from the room.

Kit let out a deep breath when she saw Mrs. Pierce. "Oh, it's you," she said.

"Whom were you expecting?" Mrs. Pierce asked.

"Randy," said Kit. "I thought he might be around here somewhere. We're sort of looking for him."

"I haven't seen him," said Mrs. Pierce. "But I did hear someone down here a few moments ago. It could have been him."

"I thought I just heard someone, too," Kit said. "I'll keep looking."

She peeked into the room behind Mrs. Pierce. Dozens of costumes hung from racks along the walls. A sewing machine sat on a table in the middle of the room. Scraps of fabric surrounded the machine.

"Isn't it kind of creepy working down here alone?" Kit asked.

"Not really," said Mrs. Pierce. "I like being alone."

Somehow this didn't surprise Kit one bit. Still, it was so dark and gloomy down there.

As if reading Kit's mind, Mrs. Pierce added, "But I do plan on bringing some of the costumes home and working on them there, too. The light's better in my sewing room at home."

"Oh, that will be nice," Kit said. She wasn't sure what to talk to Mrs. Pierce about. Usually Mom was there to keep the conversation going. Kit cleared her throat and said quickly, "Well, I still have to find Randy. I'll see you around!"

Kit gave her a lame little wave. She turned and headed back toward the steps leading up to the theater. She was only too happy to leave that creepy basement.

Where had Randy gone? Maybe he had heard Kit and just didn't feel like answering. He seemed like that kind of person.

Kit's next stop was the upstairs lobby. Randy might have helped Mrs. Greer with the memorabilia or something. As Kit walked through the theater, Mom called out to her.

"Did you find him?" she asked.

"Nope," Kit said. "I thought he might be in the lobby."

"OK," said Mom. "Go check, but hurry back."

Kit heard the familiar sound of Mooch grunting as she got closer to the lobby entrance.

"Oh brother," she muttered. If her guess was right, Mooch had pushed through the swinging lobby doors and found the treats in her backpack. When it came to finding food, Mooch was tireless. He reminded her of those bloodhounds who found missing people, only Mooch wasn't nearly as noble as they were. He'd put his big old nose to the ground and he'd sniff and sniff and sniff for clues like his life depended on it until he finally found a tiny crumb. Then—SLURP— he'd swoop that crumb into his mouth with one lick of his enormous tongue. Dad called Mooch "The Eating Machine," and it was no lie.

"Aw, Mooch!" Kit cried.

Sure enough, the first thing she saw in the lobby was Mooch sitting on her backpack with the bag of treats in his choppers. A strand of drool hung from his mouth to the floor.

"Ugh, gross," Kit whined. She bent down and dug through her backpack for a tissue. "Do you always have to drool? I mean, aren't you kind of embarrassed?"

Kit grabbed the treat bag out of Mooch's mouth and stuffed it into her backpack.

"Woof," he complained.

"Woof yourself," Kit said. "No more treats for you today." She wiped the drool off the floor with the tissue, shaking her head. "You need to learn some table manners."

Kit straightened up and scanned the lobby for a trash can to toss the tissue into. She spotted one right next to the glass display case with Gloria Canterbury's memorabilia. She started walking toward the trash can and then stopped. What was different? She stared at the display case until it dawned on her.

The Gloria Canterbury doll—the doll that cost $50,000—was gone.

# Chapter 4

# Officer Stiegler Arrives

Kit stood staring at the case. She tried walking, but her legs were as limp as noodles.

There could be a lot of reasons why the doll wasn't there. Maybe Mrs. Greer or the lady in overalls decided to take the doll out of the case for some reason. Maybe they were going to put it in its own case.

Kit forced herself to move toward the case, thinking of more reasons why the doll might not be there. Maybe it needed to be cleaned. Or they decided it was too valuable to put in the tiny little theater. After all, who would see it there? It wasn't like the theater got huge crowds or anything.

But none of those reasons seemed quite right. Kit had a seasick feeling in her stomach that told her something was wrong. Very wrong.

The glass case was closed. The empty doll stand stood in the center of the case. Nothing else had been touched—not the awards, not the silver compact, nothing. Whoever took the doll knew exactly what they wanted.

Mom was not going to be happy. Nope, she was not going to be happy at all. Kit would rather tell her that she was quitting school and joining the circus than tell her this.

"C'mon, Mooch," Kit said. "We have to go tell Mom."

Mooch whined and pulled back against his leash.

"I know. I don't want to tell her either, but we have to," Kit said.

Kit walked down the center aisle of the theater with Mooch waddling beside her.

"Did you find Randy?" Mom asked when she saw Kit and Mooch.

"Umm, no," said Kit.

"That's odd," said Mom, frowning. "Well, we've got to get going. Sorry that we couldn't find your necklace, Erika. Maybe we can keep looking for it after rehearsal today."

"Yeah, well, you won't find it until you find Randy," Erika shot back.

Mom just sighed.

"I need to talk to you," Kit said quietly. She stood in front of the stage, looking up at Mom.

Mom hopped down from the stage. "What's up?"

"I was looking for Randy in the lobby, and . . ." Kit paused.

"And?"

"Someone took the Gloria Canterbury doll."

"The what?"

Kit explained what the doll looked like and how she had spoken to Mrs. Greer earlier about it.

"Who would take a doll?" Mom asked.

"Someone who wanted $50,000," Kit replied.

It took a few seconds for the dollar amount to register in Mom's brain. But when it did, she turned as white as Morry Cheever's hair.

"I need to sit down," she said hoarsely.

Mom flopped into a seat in the front row. She looked like she had just seen something shocking, like Mooch doing a tap dance on the stage. Kit sat down beside her.

"It's only the first day of rehearsal, and things are already going so badly," Mom said, looking straight ahead.

"I was thinking that maybe Mrs. Greer decided to get the doll cleaned or something. She might have brought it back to her house for some reason."

"You think?" Mom asked. She looked like she was slowly coming out of her trance.

"Yeah," Kit said. "You should call."

"You're right. I'll call. It's probably at her house. First I'll go check it out myself," Mom said.

Mom stood, paused, and cleared her throat. "OK, why don't you all go ahead and start reading through the first act. I need to make a phone call, but I'll be right back."

Kit watched Mom leave, and then reached down and rubbed Mooch's head. "Now stay this time, OK?" she said to the old bulldog. Kit hopped onstage and joined the rest of the cast.

Kit could barely concentrate on her lines. What if someone took the doll? Mom would probably be held responsible. The play might even get cancelled. All because of a doll.

Mom came back a few minutes later, looking stunned. It was not good news—Kit just knew it.

"People, we have a problem here," Mom said. Mom looked like she had aged ten years since she left to make the telephone call. "Some time today, a very valuable doll was stolen from the case in the lobby."

Everyone started talking at once.

"What?"

"You're kidding."

"I can't believe it!"

"That was such a cool doll!"

Mom waited for everyone to settle down. Despite her calm appearance, Kit knew her mom was as nervous as a cat at a dog show.

"Did any of you take the doll out of the case for some reason?" Mom asked. "Any reason at all?"

No one responded. Mom continued, "Well, I'll have to call the police. The doll is worth a lot of money. I've already called Mrs. Greer, and she says it was here when she left. She's the only one who has a key to the case, except for me, and I lent all my keys out to Randy this morning." Mom's eyebrows squished together in an angry frown. "Where *is* that boy?"

Kit saw Morry Cheever whisper something to Sophie Gentry. She didn't need to be a lip-reader to know what they were whispering about. Now everyone would suspect Randy. And yet something way down deep in the pit of Kit's stomach told her that Randy didn't do it.

"We should all go home," Mom said, sighing. "We'll start fresh tomorrow."

"Shouldn't we be here to answer questions from the police?" Morry asked.

"Oh, sure . . . you're right," said Mom wearily. "Why don't you keep rehearsing until the police arrive."

Mom left to make the phone call to the police. As soon as she was gone, everyone started chattering.

"I can't believe it!" said Sophie. "How could so many bad things happen on the first day of rehearsal? This is not good, not good at all."

"Well, it's obvious who took it, isn't it?" asked Erika. "We all know who left mysteriously, don't we? I mean, come on, who else could it be?"

Kit shook her head. "That's not fair, Erika. It could have been anyone. We don't know what time it was taken or anything."

Erika smiled. "That's sweet that you're doing that whole 'innocent until proven guilty thing' but when you get a little older you'll realize that it's usually 'guilty until proven innocent.'"

That Erika made Kit so mad! She was about to say something to her, but Mom came back just in time.

"The police are going to be here within the next hour or so. I thought we might try to rehearse in the meantime," she said.

The cast started reading through their lines again. Morry missed two cues. Sophie complained about her lines. Erika insisted that the way she read one of her lines was perfect, even though Mom disagreed. Kit was relieved when she finally saw the police officer in the theater. The read-through was about as painful as a kick to the shins. The air was thick with tension.

The young officer had a pimply face and big, worried eyes. He took a few hesitant steps toward the stage.

"Mrs. Conroy?" he asked. His voice squeaked, like the boys in Kit's class.

"That's me," said Mom.

"I'm Officer Stiegler. I'm here to investigate the missing doll."

"Thanks for coming so quickly," Mom said. "I'll show you where the doll was kept."

Kit hopped off the stage and walked toward Mom and Officer Stiegler.

"Where do you think you're going?" Mom asked.

"I'm going with you to the crime scene," Kit said.

"Kit, this isn't a game. This is serious. Now go back and wait on the stage with the rest of the cast."

Mom spoke to her as if she were three years old, not ten. Kit opened her mouth and then closed it again, too angry to speak.

"Fine," she said finally. She leaned against the stage and pouted.

Mom and the officer disappeared through the lobby door.

"Well, I hope they find whomever did it," Morry said.

"Yeah," Holly said. She slipped a piece of gum into her mouth and chomped on it. "It's creepy thinking that a thief is wandering around the theater somewhere, stealing our stuff."

Kit didn't bother joining them on the stage. She plopped down on a seat and crossed her arms. Mom was being so unreasonable, treating her like a little kid. Kit was the one who discovered that the doll was gone. Didn't she deserve some credit?

It seemed like a decade passed before Mom came back with Officer Stiegler.

"Who was the one who saw that the doll was missing?" he asked.

Mom pointed to Kit. Officer Stiegler nodded, then looked at Kit and poised his pen over his pad of paper.

"Did you happen to notice if the display case was open or closed?" he asked.

"It was closed," Kit said.

"Was it locked?"

"I don't know. I didn't want to disturb it, so I didn't touch it," Kit replied.

Officer Stiegler looked up for the first time and grinned at her. His smile made him look even younger.

"Good thinking," he said. "It wasn't locked when I checked, but I was just wondering if you had seen it locked. Did you notice anything else unusual?"

"No, sorry," said Kit.

Officer Stiegler kept scribbling. "And who lost the necklace, the one with the horseshoe?"

"That was me," Erika said, stepping forward. She straightened her shoulders and flicked her hair. "It was a four-leaf clover, not a horseshoe," she added.

Officer Stiegler frowned, then nodded. "Sorry. I do have 'four-leaf clover' written down. I guess I just forgot. Is this necklace very valuable?"

Erika pursed her lips, then glanced at the rest of the cast in one quick sweep. "Well, not exactly," Erika said. "It's sterling silver, and has green enamel on it, but I wouldn't say it was all that valuable. It might have cost about $40, though."

Officer Stiegler briefly questioned the rest of the cast as to their whereabouts during the robberies. Then he flipped his book closed. "OK, I'll get right on this. I'll call you in a few days, Mrs. Conroy."

"Thank you, Officer," Mom said. "OK, everyone, I guess that's it for now. You can all go home and study your lines. We'll start fresh tomorrow. It's been a long day for all of us."

Kit looked at her watch. It was still early. She had time to investigate the crime scene on her own before dinner. She left the stage quietly and walked with Mooch out to the lobby. She knew if she poked around the lobby long enough, she was bound to find something—something, maybe, that proved Randy was innocent.

# Chapter 5

# The First Clue

As soon as they walked into the lobby, Mooch went straight to her backpack, just like she knew he would.

"Mooch, no. Stop that," she said, pulling him away.

Kit studied the lobby. The ticket counter was just to the left of the front door. During the season, a series of bored, unemployed actors sat in the tiny room doling out tickets, but it was too early for anyone to be there now. The door leading to the ticket booth was marked Employees Only. Kit walked over and tried the handle. Locked. She peered in through the glass at the tiny office. It had a desk and two chairs. Nothing out of the ordinary there.

The snack machine, which was stocked with stale candy bars and potato chips, was across from ticket window. Next to it stood the soda machine and a few folding chairs. Her backpack was on one of the chairs and her scooter was behind it. The only other things in the lobby were the glass case against the opposite wall, a wastepaper basket, and a phone booth. Mom had told her they planned on roping off the area in front of the case and displaying other stuff behind the rope, like one of Gloria's old dresses and maybe her old trunk. Kit thought it was a terrible idea. The lobby was crowded enough as it was, especially during intermissions, when the audience came out to buy the stale candy bars and talk about the show.

Next to the case was an old radiator. In the winter it banged away so loudly that sometimes you could hear it in the theater, but now, in the dead of summer, it was quiet.

Kit stepped closer to the glass case. Inside, Kit saw the gloves, the silver compact, the brush and comb set, the black-and-white photos, the awards, and the empty doll stand.

Whoever took the doll knew it was valuable. How would Randy know this? Even though the doll looked kind of cool, Kit never would have guessed it was worth so much. She doubted that Randy had a doll collection at home or any knowledge of dolls at all.

But Erika did.

Erika had admired the doll. She said it was the most beautiful thing she had ever seen, or something like that.

Kit stared at the case, thinking, until the sound of Mooch's whining startled her out of her thoughts.

"I told you, no more treats," she said.

When Mooch looked at her with those big brown eyes, he was hard to resist.

"OK, just one," Kit said, digging through her backpack. "Here." She tossed him a treat. He gobbled it up in a second.

Kit, still crouching by her backpack, took another look around. Things looked different from Mooch's point of view. That was for sure. She could see candy bar wrappers under the radiator.

And something else. Something shiny. Maybe it was just a piece of tinfoil. Kit grabbed a tissue and crawled on her hands and knees over to the radiator. Mooch watched her with a funny look on his face, as if to say, "Since when did you turn into a dog?"

The closer Kit got, the more certain she was that this was not a piece of tinfoil. It wasn't as shiny, for one thing. And it wasn't all crumpled up. She held her breath, reached under the dusty old radiator, and grabbed it with the tissue.

It was hard and cool, as if it were made of metal. Kit uncurled her fingers and studied it.

A slim silver cylinder lay in the palm of her hand. A red jewel glimmered on the top of it and the initials

"GC" were scrolled in fancy letters along the side. Using the tissue, Kit pulled it open. A bullet-shaped glob of bright red lipstick surprised her. It was a lipstick case! A fancy-schmancy lipstick case that only a movie star would carry.

Kit turned it around, examining it from all sides. The bottom had "sterling silver" stamped on it. Kit guessed that the jewel on top was a garnet. Her grandmother had an old-fashioned picture frame in her house with the same type of red jewel on

top of it. Grams had told Kit it was a garnet, Kit's birthstone, and that's why she put Kit's picture in it. The red jewel on the lipstick case looked just like the garnet in the picture frame.

The lipstick case probably belonged to Gloria Canterbury, and yet Kit couldn't remember seeing it in the display case. She looked at the items there—the brush and comb set and the compact. They were also silver, but none of them had garnets on them. They weren't inscribed with the initials "GC", either.

Perhaps the lady with the overalls had dropped the lipstick case and didn't know it. There was certainly a lot of commotion earlier this morning. But wouldn't Mrs. Greer realize that the lipstick case never made it into the glass case? Or had the thief, whomever it was, tried to steal this, too, and then dropped it when he or she heard someone coming? They might have grabbed whatever they saw first, which was the doll, and then saw the lipstick case—wherever it was—and grabbed that, too. When they dropped the lipstick case it rolled under the radiator and there was no time to retrieve it.

Kit stared at the sterling silver case in her hand. Who had held it last? And was that the answer to the mystery?

Kit heard the lobby door opening behind her. She spun around and saw Erika.

"What are you doing?" Erika asked, stepping closer. "Hey, what's that?"

Kit held the case up to Erika and watched her face closely. "I found it under the radiator. I think the doll thief might have dropped it."

Erika looked puzzled, but not exactly nervous. Then again, she was an actress. She could be nervous and Kit would never know. Actresses hide their nervousness all the time.

"What is it?" Erika asked.

"It's a lipstick case." Kit opened it so Erika could see the bright red lipstick inside.

"Cool," said Erika. "What's that along the side?"

"The initials 'GC'," Kit said.

"Wow, that must have been Gloria Canterbury's!" Erika exclaimed. "Can I hold it?"

Kit held it out to her using the tissue. Erika gingerly took the lipstick case from Kit.

"It's so beautiful," she said. "And so glamorous! That Gloria Canterbury was soooo cool."

"I never could get through that movie she was in. It was so boring," Kit argued.

"Boring?" Erika looked at Kit with disgust. "That was one of the most brilliant performances I've ever seen."

Kit shrugged. "I still thought it was boring."

"Oh no, it was perfect," Erika said in a soft voice. "She is my favorite actress. When she tilts her chin up and looks defiantly into the camera—well, there is nobody who does it better."

Who knew Erika was such a Gloria Canterbury nut? A devoted fan like that would probably do anything for some memorabilia. Anything.

The lobby door opened again and Mom poked her head in.

"What are you two doing?" Mom asked.

"I found this under the radiator," Kit said, taking the case and the tissue from Erika's hand and walking it over to Mom. "I think the thief tried to steal it but got scared or startled or something and then dropped it."

"Hmm," Mom said. She turned the case around using the tissue. "I don't remember seeing it before, but then I only looked at the case briefly this morning. Mrs. Greer might have added other things later, though, without my knowing it. We'd better mention it to the police."

"Do you think I could keep it in the meantime?" Kit asked. She figured that having the evidence so nearby might help her solve the case.

"OK, but take it home and put it in a safe place," Mom said, handing the lipstick case back to Kit. "I'll take it to Officer Stiegler as soon as I can."

Kit glanced outside and saw that the sun was going down. If she raced home she might be able to catch Spencer online. He had said he'd be on between 5:00 and 6:00.

"Come on, Mooch, we have to hustle," she said. She tugged him toward the door. "See you at home," she called to Mom.

When Kit got home, it was ten minutes to six.

She logged on right away and punched in her password. Seconds later, the Instant Message window popped open.

> **Segreti410:** Where've you been? I was just about to log off.
>
> **StarGirl:** You won't believe this! You just won't believe it!
>
> **Segreti410:** What, what?

There was so much to tell him! Where should she begin? Kit drummed the keyboard lightly, thinking.

> **Segreti410:** Helloooooo?
>
> **StarGirl:** OK, OK, hold on. First of all, there was a robbery today at the theater. Wait—two robberies, now that I think of it!
>
> **Segreti410:** Get out!
>
> **StarGirl:** I'm out! First, this girl named Erika had a four-leaf-clover necklace stolen. THEN a Gloria Canterbury doll was stolen. All in one day!
>
> **Segreti410:** What's the big deal about some doll being stolen?
>
> **StarGirl:** This isn't just "some doll." This doll costs—are you ready?
>
> **Segreti410:** Yeah, I'm ready.
>
> **StarGirl:** Are you sure?
>
> **Segreti410:** Quit with the drama and just tell me!
>
> **StarGirl:** $50,000!

Kit could imagine Spencer's mouth falling open. He finally responded moments later.

**Segreti410:** HOW MUCH?

Kit giggled.

**StarGirl:** You read right. $50,000!
**Segreti410:** Who would pay $50,000 for a doll?
**StarGirl:** A doll collector, I guess.

The Instant Message box was blank for a few seconds. Kit knew Spencer loved a mystery. He had read every Hardy Boy mystery, every Encyclopedia Brown book, and was now on to Agatha Christie mysteries. He was absolutely the perfect person to talk to about this.

**Segreti410:** Who do you think did it?
**StarGirl:** I thought you'd never ask. OK, first there's Erika, the lead in the play. She's my number one suspect. She has a doll collection at home, and she was offstage when the crime might have occurred.
**Segreti410:** Might have occurred?
**StarGirl:** Well, yeah. I don't know EXACTLY when the doll was taken. I THINK it was taken sometime after 2:00 and sometime before 3:00. The last time I saw it was at 2:00. I know that for sure

because rehearsals start at 2:00 on Saturdays, so that's when I got to the theater and saw it being put into the display case.

**Segreti410:** What happened next? What was going on between 2:00 and 3:00?

Kit told him all about the screaming and the necklace and about Randy. By the end of her story, her fingers were sore.

**Segreti410:** So you don't think Randy took it?

Kit shook her head, as if Spencer were in the room with her.

**StarGirl:** Nope! I really don't. I mean, think about it. This is a doll we're talking about. Do you really think any young guy would steal a doll? Or even a cheap necklace? And Randy never would have guessed that the doll cost so much. Never in a billion years would anyone have guessed that it was worth $50,000.

**Segreti410:** Good point. OK, who else might have taken it? We need suspects and motives.

Kit sat back in her chair and looked up at her dusty light fixture on the ceiling. Was anyone else missing? She had been so sure it was Erika. The rest of the cast was on stage with her. Morry, Sophia, Holly, Jeff . . . Wait.

**StarGirl:** Mrs. Pierce! I bumped into her in the basement when I was looking for Randy. She might have been in the lobby when the crime happened. There's a door that goes outside from the basement. She could have sneaked out, then sneaked back into the basement after she took the doll.

**Segreti401:** What's her motive?

Kit stared at her ceiling again, frowning.

**StarGirl:** She doesn't really like my mom at all. She might be trying to sabotage the whole play.

**Segreti410:** Well, you know what you have to do now, don't you?

**StarGirl:** No. What?

**Segreti410:** You have to investigate, Sherlock. And if I were you, I'd start hunting around in that basement for the doll.

**StarGirl:** Ugh. I HATE it down there.

**Segreti410:** Hey, if you really want to clear Randy's name, you're going to have to do some investigating.

He was right, of course. He was right 99.9999 percent of the time. She kind of hated him for that.

**StarGirl:** OK. I'll keep you up-to-date. Let's try to keep meeting here at this time, OK?

**Segreti410:** Deal. Good luck.

Kit bit her lip. Did Erika steal the doll to add it to her collection? Was it possible that Mrs. Pierce took it to sabotage the play? And how easy would it be to find the doll in that old basement? Kit wondered. She had the feeling she was going to need a lot of luck.

# Chapter 6

# A Threat Is Made

Sunday rehearsals were held at 3:00. Kit hung out in her room that morning, calling friends and listening to her CDs, waiting until it was time to leave for the theater. When it was time, Kit stood in the front hall and put on her helmet and protective gear. Mooch stood by her side.

"You're not bringing Mooch again, are you?" Mom asked.

"Why not? He didn't do anything wrong yesterday. Besides, he gets so lonely without me."

Mom sighed and shook her head. "Kit, I'm trying to make this play go smoothly, and yet every time I turn around, you're disrupting it."

"Me? How?"

"Well, you brought Mooch, for one thing. You talked back to Erika, who was already distressed enough as it was. And then you expected me to let you play detective with that police officer. Honestly, Kit, I don't know what to do with you."

Kit stared at Mom. She looked pale and worn out.

It just didn't seem worth arguing about anything when Mom looked so exhausted, even though Kit thought everything she said was totally unfair.

"I'm sorry, Mom. I don't mean to be messing things up for you. But Erika was accusing Randy of stealing! Without any proof! I couldn't just let her get away with it."

Mooch grunted in agreement, which made them both laugh.

"I guess you think Erika was wrong, too, huh Mooch?" Mom asked.

Kit knelt down and hugged Mooch. "Mooch won't do anything wrong, Mom," she pleaded.

Mooch licked his big chops and looked straight at Mom, as if he knew exactly what they were talking about.

Mom smiled. "OK, you can bring him. But if he makes any trouble at all, he's out."

Kit grinned and gave Mom a hug. She raced out the door with Mooch, grabbed her scooter from behind the bushes, and headed toward the theater. Mooch huffed alongside her.

People were already bustling around when Kit got there. Mrs. Pierce was fitting Holly for her costume. Erika and Sophie rehearsed a scene in one corner of the stage while Jeff and Morry rehearsed in another corner. Stew Baker was on a ladder, adjusting a light.

Mom had called Stew, who ran the hardware store in town, to help out with the props and the scenery until Randy came back. Kit looked for Randy, but didn't see him anywhere.

"Did Randy ever show up?" she asked Holly, who was practicing her lines.

Holly shook her head. "Nope. No one has heard from him, either. It's so weird."

"Yeah," Kit said. "That is weird."

Mom rushed in a few minutes after Kit, her auburn hair flying behind her.

"Sorry I'm late, everyone," she said, breathing heavily.

She was only about two minutes late, but Kit decided not to argue with her.

"OK, before we begin, I'd like to thank you all for staying yesterday and answering questions from the police. I hope the doll and Erika's necklace show up soon," Mom told the group.

"So do I," Erika said.

Kit rolled her eyes. Luckily, Mom didn't see her do it, but Erika did. She shot Kit a killer look.

"How are the costumes coming along, Leslie?" Mom asked Mrs. Pierce.

"Fine. I've finished Kit's. Would you like to see it?"

"Oh my, that's exciting!" Mom said. "Thanks for working so quickly! I'd love to see it!"

Mrs. Pierce left the stage and came back moments later holding a hanger with Kit's costume on it.

Kit stared hard at the costume. It looked awfully small. Like it was made for a little kid, not a fourth grader.

"Hmm," said Mom. The lines between her eyebrows grew deeper as she studied the costume. "Why don't you try on the jacket, Kit, so we can see how it looks."

Kit held her breath. There was no way that costume would fit her. No way on Earth. Couldn't Mrs. Pierce see that?

But Mrs. Pierce seemed not to notice the small size of the jacket. She slipped it off the hanger and held it out for Kit to try on.

Kit looked at Mom, who nodded, as if to say, "Go ahead, try it on." So Kit shrugged and daintily snaked her right arm into the right sleeve. The sleeve squeezed her arm tightly. When Kit tried to put her left arm in, she couldn't do it. There wasn't enough room. The jacket would barely fit a five-year-old, much less a ten-year-old.

"Umm, it doesn't fit," Kit said.

"Of course it fits. I took the measurements," said

Mrs. Pierce. She took Kit's left arm and tried twisting it behind her back so that it would fit into the sleeve.

"It *really* doesn't fit, Mrs. Pierce," Kit said, pulling her arm away.

The lines between Mom's eyebrows were as deep as the Grand Canyon by now. "Leslie, what happened? How could you be so wrong about the measurements?"

Uh-oh. This was not good. Not good at all. Kit had been on the receiving end of Mom's edgy mood for the past 24 hours, and it wasn't fun. She knew just how Mrs. Pierce felt.

Mrs. Pierce was not going to take it, Kit could see. She gave Mom an icy cold stare.

"I'm sorry that I'm human," she said, sniffing. "I'm sorry that I made one tiny mistake." Mrs. Pierce threw Kit's costume on the floor before she stormed off.

The cast had all heard the exchange by now. Everyone waited to see what Mom would do.

Mom sighed loudly. She rubbed her temples in that circular pattern that she had grown so fond of lately. If she kept doing that, Kit was sure she'd rub her skin right off.

"OK, people, let's rehearse the first scene. Kit, since you're not in the scene, would you run down to

Mrs. Pierce's sewing room and have her measure you again?" Mom asked.

Seeing Mrs. Pierce in the mood she was in now was not something Kit wanted to do. But maybe while she was down there, she could do some serious snooping.

"OK," Kit said.

She hopped off the stage and walked quickly down the aisle to the lobby.

"Where are you going?" Mom asked. "The door to the basement is the other way."

"Ummm, I've got to go to the bathroom," Kit called. "I'll be right back."

Walking past the stage, Kit listened to Mom giving Erika directions on how to read one of her lines.

"I just don't get the sense that you're really frightened," Mom said. "Try thinking of a time when you were really scared. How did you feel?"

Erika blew her bangs away from her face and scowled. "But I *did* feel scared when I said that line! Couldn't you hear my voice shaking? I mean, how much more scared do you want me to be?"

Kit knew that Mom had a problem with touchy actors. She was always complaining about one of the actors on the sitcom she starred in. She said that even though the director was almost always right, this actor argued with him over every line. Mom said it drained the director of his energy for the other actors.

In this case Mom was being drained by just about everyone! Kit vowed that she would try being more cooperative with Mom.

When Mooch saw Kit walk by, he got up from his napping spot and walked toward her.

"C'mon, Mooch," Kit said, "let's go see Mrs. Pierce."

Kit gave him a quick scratch behind the ears before heading toward the basement. When she got to the top of the stairs she paused and looked down. The basement seemed to get darker and creepier each time she visited it. The moldy, damp smell was nearly overwhelming. Kit inched her way down the stairs, holding her nose.

Kit was about to call out to Mrs. Pierce when she heard someone talking. She followed the voice, tiptoeing down the narrow hallway, until she came to the costume room. Kit stood outside, listening.

"Who does she think she is, the queen of England?" Mrs. Pierce said. Kit heard her pacing back and forth on the basement's cement floor. "Here I am, working my fingers to the bone, and all she can do is complain."

Kit waited to hear what the other person in the room would say, but whoever it was stayed quiet.

"It took me hours to make that costume! Hours! I bet it would fit if that spoiled little girl would just give it a try."

Spoiled little girl? Was she talking about Kit?

"But I suppose if Pamela Conroy wants a new costume, Pamela Conroy will get it. Just like she gets everything else she wants."

Kit could feel that familiar burn in her cheeks again. Her mom didn't *just* get everything she wanted! She worked hard for all the good things that came her way, and she rarely complained.

And that "spoiled little girl" comment was totally uncalled for, too!

Kit could hear Mrs. Pierce pacing back and forth and throwing papers around. She decided to peek into the room to see how the other person was reacting to Mrs. Pierce. She stuck her head into the room and quickly looked around.

But there was no one else there. Just Mrs. Pierce, talking to herself.

"She's going to be sorry she ever humiliated me that way in front of the whole cast," Mrs. Pierce said, her back to Kit. "Very, very sorry."

# Chapter 7

# A Reward Is Offered

Kit stood there without moving while her heart beat wildly in her chest. What Mrs. Pierce had said made Kit shaky. Kit had never before realized how much Mrs. Pierce disliked Mom. She remembered Mom saying that Mrs. Pierce was a little jealous of her, but this was more than just a little jealous. This was jealousy in its brightest shade of green.

Kit was not about to be fitted for her costume with Mrs. Pierce in such a dark mood. Kit tiptoed back down the hall and up the stairs. By the time she arrived at the stage, her heartbeat was normal again, but her hands were still shaky. It was creepy thinking of Mrs. Pierce in the dark, smelly basement all by herself. Really creepy.

"Are you all set with your costume?" Mom asked.

"Um, no, Mrs. Pierce looked sort of busy, so I didn't bother her," Kit said.

Mom frowned. "Well, just be sure to get down there sometime soon for a fitting."

Rehearsal dragged on. Erika argued with everything Mom said. Morry goofed up half of his lines. Even Kit, who normally loved rehearsing, felt like she wasn't all there. She couldn't concentrate on her lines or how she was supposed to move on the stage. She kept exiting stage right instead of stage left. All she could think about was Mrs. Pierce and what she had said about Mom. Could Mrs. Pierce have stolen the doll, just to ruin Mom's debut as a director? It seemed possible. That was for sure.

Midway through rehearsal, Mrs. Greer strutted down the aisle wearing a kelly green suit. Everything stopped.

65

The cast stared at her.

"Hello, Mrs. Greer," Mom said, her voice cracking. "Can we help you with something?"

Mrs. Greer seemed just as chipper as she was when Kit first met her, despite the missing doll. She smiled and waved to everyone.

"Hello, Pamela, so good to see you. I heard a few lines from your show and it sounds wonderful. Good job," Mrs. Greer said.

Mom glanced down at the floor, shifting from one foot to the other. "Well, thank you," she murmured.

"But I am a little distressed about this missing doll. My aunt was quite fond of that doll. And it is, as you know, very valuable."

"We did call the police," Mom said. "I know they'll do everything they can."

"I don't doubt that," Mrs. Greer said, smiling at Mom. "But I think we could all use—how shall I say it—a little bit of encouragement? I am prepared to offer a reward of $1,000 to anyone who can find my aunt's doll."

Kit gasped. A $1,000 reward! She could think of about a billion things she could do with all that money. Like maybe buy a new bicycle, and a new doggie bed for Mooch, and even a new baseball mitt.

The list went on and on. She could barely pay attention to what Mom and Mrs. Greer were saying.

"That's very generous of you, Mrs. Greer," Mom said, "but I don't think . . ."

Mrs. Greer waved her hand in the air. "Oh, don't worry about the police and what they'll think of this. Just try to retrieve that doll. I won't be able to sleep at night knowing that it's not in its proper place. My aunt wanted to give back to the community, and I'd like to help her do just that."

"Well, I certainly hope we find the doll soon," Mom said.

"Mrs. Greer, was anything else missing from the display case?" Kit piped in.

"No, dear, just the doll, thank goodness," Mrs. Greer replied. "Why do you ask?"

"Oh, just wondering," said Kit.

"If you do find the doll, please call me right away." Mrs. Greer smiled her cheerful smile. "Well, don't let me keep you from your rehearsal. Good luck, everyone!"

A few people mumbled their thanks while Mrs. Greer bustled up the aisle and through the lobby door.

"I hope you all haven't forgotten about *my* necklace," Erika said.

"How could we forget?" Kit asked. "You bring it up every ten seconds."

Holly snickered. Mom shot Kit a dirty look.

"Well, just because I can't afford a big reward doesn't mean the necklace isn't important. I've always worn that necklace to rehearsals and I've never performed without it. If we don't get that necklace back, this play is doomed. I just know it!" Erika said dramatically.

That topped Kit's list of the Dumbest Things Ever Said. Like a necklace had anything to do with a good performance. As if!

But what if the two thefts were somehow related? Mrs. Pierce could be angry at Mom and trying—in her weird way—to sabotage the show by stealing all these things. If the actors start thinking the play is doomed, then Mrs. Pierce will have won.

Kit just had to find that doll. If not for the money, then at least for Mom. Kit couldn't stop thinking about it all through rehearsal.

"Kit, where are you?" Mom asked her, after Kit missed her cue for the second time.

"Sorry," she replied. "I guess I'm having trouble concentrating today."

"Please start paying better attention," Mom said. She turned to the rest of the cast. "We all need to pull together if we're going to put this show on. I know a lot has happened, but we can't let that get in the way of this performance, OK?"

A few heads nodded.

"Sorry," Kit mumbled. "I'll try harder."

But it was hard to concentrate when a thief was in their midst.

Later that night, Mom made her infamous macaroni and cheese, with Kit's help. They discussed the play and the actors, as usual, while Mooch stood around waiting for someone to drop food on the floor.

"Erika's doing well, don't you think?" Mom asked.

"Ugh. She argues with everything you say."

"I'm not always right, you know."

Kit couldn't help but wonder why Mom always seemed to think she was right when she argued with *her*.

"I think she's upset about that necklace of hers," Mom said kindly.

"Well, I'm sick of hearing about that necklace. And I'm sick of the way she keeps pinning the theft on Randy. There's absolutely no proof that he took that necklace," said Kit.

Mom tossed the salad while Kit set the kitchen table. Kit thought Mom should know about Mrs. Pierce and how she acted in the costume room, but

69

she wasn't sure how Mom would take it.

"What's the deal with Mrs. Pierce?" Kit asked.

"What do you mean?" Mom asked. She took a bite of her macaroni and cheese and then added more salt.

"Why is she so jealous of you?"

Mom turned the stove off. She paused before speaking.

"Years ago, she and I were up for the same role in an important play. I got the part, she didn't. It was just a silly little part, but I guess it really affected her. She stopped acting after that," Mom explained.

"Wow. She stopped acting?"

Mom shrugged. "I felt really bad at first, but then I figured if she let something like that get in her way, then she really wasn't cut out for a career in acting. You can't let rejection get you down in this business, Kit. Remember that."

Kit was about to tell Mom about how strangely Mrs. Pierce was acting in the costume room when the phone rang.

Mom sighed. "Who could that be?"

"Don't answer it," said Kit. "It's probably just some guy trying to sell you a magazine subscription."

"Yes, but it could be Dad, too," Mom said, getting up.

The last time Dad called, he still hadn't found a dog or cat that could wash dishes. Somehow his problems seemed pretty small compared to theirs.

Kit concentrated on putting the food out on the table. She wasn't really paying attention to Mom's conversation until she heard her say, *What?*

Kit spun around and looked at Mom, whose mouth had dropped open.

"Just see what you can do about it, OK, Stew?" Mom said. She hung up the phone and then stared at it for a second, as if the telephone had suddenly come alive and was singing a Broadway show tune.

"What's wrong?" Kit asked.

"That was Stew Baker," Mom said.

"Yeah?"

"You know those big, expensive floor pillows we were going to use as props? The ones Randy found for us? The ones that were just perfect for that first scene?" Mom asked.

"I think so," Kit said. She wasn't sure she wanted to hear the rest of the story.

"Well, they're gone," Mom said. "Someone took them from the prop room."

Kit didn't know what to say.

"What next?" Mom said, rubbing her temples.

# Chapter 8

# Costume Calamity

Days passed. Each rehearsal seemed to drag on like an eternity. No matter what Mom said or did, no one seemed able to concentrate.

One sunny afternoon, Kit and Mooch arrived at rehearsal a few minutes early. The only other person in the theater was Erika. For a second, Kit considered waiting outside the theater for rehearsal to begin. It was a golden summer afternoon. Birds chirped like crazy in the trees and a lawnmower spread the scent of freshly cut grass from the yard next door. She hated to ruin a perfectly good day by getting into an argument with Erika. Then she thought of Spencer, who would certainly tell her that the only way to figure this whole thing out was to talk to people. So she took a deep breath, reminded herself not to lose her temper, and strode up to Erika, who was sitting on a folding chair onstage, studying her script. Erika's bulging purse was plunked in front of her feet. Kit could see a cell phone antenna sticking up out of it.

"Hey," Kit said, as cheerfully as she could manage.

Erika looked up from her script. "Hello," she said stiffly. She went back to reading her script, as though Kit wasn't even there.

Kit decided she would have to take drastic measures to make Erika talk to her.

"I think you did a great job with that second act yesterday. Really brilliant," Kit said.

Erika frowned. "Really?"

"Oh yeah. It was perfect the way you tossed your head back like that. Just perfect."

Erika smiled. Kit was surprised at how pretty she looked when she smiled. "I thought that was good, too. Your mom didn't think so, though."

Kit dismissed that with a wave of her hand.

"No, your mom was probably right," Erika said as she stared off to her right. "I don't know why I always argue with her," she said softly. "I guess I just want her to think my performance is perfect. I have so much respect for her."

Kit couldn't believe what she was hearing. She wished Mom were there to hear it. But somehow she thought Mom might already know how Erika felt.

"Yeah, well, sometimes she's wrong, trust me," Kit said. She squatted next to Mooch and rubbed his big belly. Without looking at Erika, she continued, "And I'm sure you're feeling like things aren't going that great now, with your necklace missing and all."

Erika stood up. "Yeah, you're right." She grabbed her purse. "I have to make a phone call."

Erika moved as fast as if she were running the 50-yard dash. Within seconds she disappeared into the lobby.

"Wow," Kit whispered to Mooch. "What was that all about?"

If Erika really needed to make a phone call that badly, why didn't she just use her cell phone? Even if she wanted some privacy, you'd think she'd just take it to another corner of the stage or something.

Kit had the funny feeling Erika was lying about the phone call. But why?

Soon the other cast members trickled in. Kit had given up hope about Randy. He was gone. That was all there was to it.

Kit watched Erika closely throughout rehearsal. Whenever Mom told her something, she actually seemed to listen. She didn't argue once.

What had made her change? Any change in behavior made Kit suspicious.

Halfway through the third act, Mrs. Pierce showed up. She stood in front of the stage, waiting for Mom to address her.

"What's up, Leslie?" Mom asked, the beginnings

of a frown edging around her mouth and eyes.

"I'm afraid I have some bad news," Mrs. Pierce said. "It's very bad," she added.

Kit could hear Mom take a big breath. "OK. I'm ready. What is it?"

Mrs. Pierce's eye twitched. "Um, well, I brought the costumes home yesterday to work on them." She paused. Her eye twitched so badly it looked like it might pop out of her head.

"And?" Mom asked.

"I've been working on them in my basement, and, well, it flooded yesterday. The costumes are all ruined. I'm sorry."

"What?" Mom demanded. "All of them? Every single costume is ruined?"

"Yes," Mrs. Pierce said. "I'm sorry. I guess the show won't be able to go on. And I'm truly sorry about that. Really, I am. If there was anything I could do, I would, but I can't."

Mom held her face in her hands and shook her head. "I don't believe this," she mumbled. "I just don't believe it."

Mom was about to have a major meltdown right in front of the entire cast. Kit knew it. "Mom," Kit said, "maybe you'd better sit down."

"This is no time for sitting, Kit. This is a time for

thinking and acting!" Mom snapped at her.

"Whoa," Kit said, taking a step backward.

Mom clenched her jaw. Kit decided it was probably better to keep her mouth shut for a while.

"OK," Mom said, "let's think what we can do."

The cast was silent. After a few seconds, Holly asked, "How did your basement flood, Mrs. Pierce? It didn't rain last night."

Kit thought that was an excellent question. Everyone turned to Mrs. Pierce.

Mrs. Pierce cleared her throat. "A pipe burst," she said. More eye twitches.

"Do you wear contact lenses?" Kit asked abruptly.

"No, why?" Mrs. Pierce asked.

"Your eye keeps twitching, like you've got dust in your lens or something. I was just wondering," Kit said innocently.

"Can we stop with the small talk and get back to our problem, folks?" Mom asked.

Kit studied the floor, thinking. Mrs. Pierce and her twitching eye troubled her. Mrs. Pierce sure was acting guilty. Did she purposely ruin the costumes? Just to get revenge on Mom? It seemed too mean to be true.

"Maybe we could rent costumes," Morry said.

"That would be much too expensive, Morry," Mom said. "We have a very tight budget as it is."

"Isn't there some way we could salvage the costumes, Mrs. Pierce?" Holly asked. "We could wash them or . . ."

"No," Mrs. Pierce interrupted, "there's nothing we can do. I should know. I've been sewing costumes for 20 years. I'm sorry."

"What if we were all in charge of our own costume?" Erika asked. "People could rent a costume, or they could make their own, depending on how much they wanted to spend."

Mom's face brightened. "Now, *that's* a good idea. Thank you, Erika."

Erika grinned at Mom and then looked down at the floor.

"What does everyone think?" Mom asked.

"I think it's a horrible idea," Mrs. Pierce said. "The costumes will look as though they were just thrown together. Some might be of high quality, but others will be poorly made. And everyone will think I made them all!"

Mom shook her head. "I really don't see what else we can do."

"You can cancel the production," Mrs. Pierce said. "Everything is going so terribly that it will certainly be for the best."

Mom crossed her arms. "I have never, ever

cancelled a production in my entire career, and I don't intend to start now. I'm one of those people who believes the show must go on." She stared at the cast defiantly. "I think we can do it. What do you all say?"

Everyone cheered. Mom smiled. It was the first time Kit had seen her smile in days.

"If that's the case, I don't want to have anything to do with this play," Mrs. Pierce said. She turned her back on the cast and stormed out of the theater.

"Let's continue with the rehearsal," Mom said. "Where were we?"

For the rest of rehearsal, Mom criticized everything about Kit's performance, right down to the way she walked on stage.

"I'm trying my best!" Kit said to her.

"It's just not as good as it can be, Kit," Mom replied.

After rehearsal, Mom slipped her arm around Kit. "Was I too hard on you today?" she asked.

"Yes!" Kit said.

"Sorry, it's just that I know you can do better. You're a very good actress, Kit."

"It's just a community play, Mom. It's not Broadway!"

Mom looked like she was about to say something to Kit and then changed her mind.

"C'mon," she said, "I need to look over the budget. Why don't you and Mooch come down and keep me company?"

All three went down to the basement to the director's office. Being down there with Mom made the basement seem a little less scary, but not much.

Mom's tiny office was crammed with papers. Theater posters from past productions hung on the yellowed walls. Three half-empty coffee mugs sat on Mom's desk next to an ancient computer. A blue sticky note was stuck to the side of it, which read "Missing more props: stool and blanket for second act. Stew."

"More props missing," Mom muttered. "What is going on?"

Kit plopped down on the old stuffed sofa. Mooch hopped up next to her.

"I almost forgot," Mom said, pulling the *Edgeview Clarion* out of a stack of papers. "There's an article about the play. Your name is in it."

"Really?" Kit asked. "Cool."

Kit grabbed the paper from Mom and scanned the article. At the top of the page was a picture of Mrs. Greer in front of the theater. Underneath the picture it read, "Mrs. Gertrude Greer, niece of the legendary actress Gloria Canterbury, in front of the newly renovated Gloria Canterbury Theater." It was a nice picture of Mrs. Greer, who was smiling that friendly smile of hers. Halfway down the article the reporter listed the cast members.

"There's my name!" Kit said, pointing to it. She giggled.

"How does it feel?" Mom asked.

"Great!"

"How about celebrating your first time in print with a couple of sodas?" Mom dug into her purse.

Edgeview Clarion

Community Events

Theater News

Mrs. Gertrude Gr
the legendary G
in front of the
Gloria Cante

"Here," she said, handing Kit some change. "Get yourself a candy bar, too."

"Thanks!" Kit said. "Come on, Mooch."

Kit and Mooch wandered down the long hall that led to the stairs that went up to the stage and the lobby. Suddenly Kit was aware of a buttery smell that she had never smelled in the basement before.

"Who's making popcorn?" she asked Mooch. She looked to her left. A door was cracked open. Kit opened it more and peered in. It lead to another door at the end of a long hallway.

The popcorn smell was even stronger.

"Come on, Mooch," she said. "This is weird."

Kit walked three steps, then stopped. She could hear other footsteps coming from the end of the dark hallway.

"Is someone there?" she asked.

Just then the lights went out. Kit was in total darkness.

# Chapter 9

# Follow That Suspect!

Kit froze. Mooch whined beside her.

"Shh, Mooch, quiet," she whispered.

Kit heard someone walking very slowly at the end of the hallway. Instead of walking toward her, they seemed to be walking away from her.

"Let's get out of here, boy," she said.

Kit felt along the walls with her hands, trying to make her way back to Mom, but she couldn't even tell if she was going in the right direction. As she walked, the popcorn smell became fainter and fainter. It was so quiet that all she could hear was Mooch's toenails clicking on the cement floor.

"Kit?" Mom called.

"I'm here!" Kit said. Her voice quivered.

"I can't believe how dark it is in here. Oh, wait, I think this is the door to the outside," Mom said.

Kit heard the heavy door creak open. The early evening light was just enough for them to see by.

"What happened?" Mom asked, giving Kit a quick hug.

"I don't know," Kit said. "First I smelled popcorn, then the lights went out."

"I don't like this one bit," Mom said. She ushered Kit through the door with Mooch at her heels. "Come on, let's go."

Kit decided to leave her scooter and her backpack in the lobby for the night. She could always get there early the next day to pick them up. There was no way she was going back into the theater. Not with some crazy, popcorn-loving person wandering around in the basement.

As soon as she got home, Kit raced up to her bedroom to tell Spencer everything that happened.

"Please, Spencer, be online," she whispered as she typed in her password.

Her buddy list showed that Spencer was still online. Within seconds he was sending her an Instant Message.

**Segreti410:** OK, Nancy Drew, what's happening with your mystery?

Kit typed furiously, filling him in on everything that had happened in the past few days. She told him about Mrs. Greer's reward money, the ruined costumes, and the popcorn smell in the basement.

> **StarGirl:** And now, suddenly, Erika is acting really nice to Mom. She didn't argue once with her in rehearsal today.
>
> **Segreti410:** I think she has the strongest motive since she has that doll collection at home.
>
> **StarGirl:** Yeah, but what about that necklace of hers? That was taken, too.
>
> **Segreti410:** Maybe it wasn't. Maybe she only "pretended" it was taken so that it would throw everyone off track.

Kit hadn't thought of that, but it made perfect sense.

> **Segreti410:** You've got to follow her. See if she does anything mysterious.

Kit snorted.

> **StarGirl:** I can't think of anything more boring than that. No, wait, watching golf on TV. That might be more boring, but not much.
>
> **Segreti410:** Look, do you want to solve this mystery or not?

Kit rolled her eyes.

> **StarGirl:** You're right. I'll start following her. But it's going to be B-O-R-I-N-G, trust me.

That night, while eating Chinese food right out of the containers, Kit asked Mom where Erika lived.

"Oh, she lives on Beaumont, in a green house just around the corner. I gave her a ride home after rehearsal the other night. Why do you ask?"

"No reason, really. Guess I'm just curious about her."

"Hmmm," Mom said, "that's interesting."

Kit just shrugged. Tomorrow she would start Operation Erika.

After two days of following Erika around, Kit was about to give up. Erika's life was just as boring as Kit thought it would be. After working part-time at Chic-Chic, a trendy little store in town, Erika would spend the afternoon shopping until it was time for rehearsal. Dullsville.

Kit complained to Spencer at night, but he kept urging her to stay with it, saying that she was bound to discover something interesting.

Then, on the third day, something did happen. Erika walked to work that day with a brown paper bag under her arm. It was too big to be lunch, and the bag wasn't from some ritzy store in town. It was just an ordinary brown bag, which made it that much more mysterious. Erika never carried anything ordinary.

After work, Erika started down the block, but not in her usual direction. Instead of going toward the trendy shops and restaurants, she was heading in the other direction where the dry cleaners, the Mini Mart, the shoe repair, and an antique shop were located.

When Kit saw the antique shop, her heart started pounding so fast it felt like it was going to burst.

In the window were dolls. Lots of dolls. Old, beat-up dolls in dusty clothes and fancier dolls wearing velvet dresses were lined up in the window, some of them sitting in doll-sized chairs. A sign read "Antique Doll Month. Come See Our Collection!"

And here was Erika bringing a mysterious paper bag to the shop! Could she be bringing in the Gloria Canterbury doll?

As soon as Erika walked through the door, Kit moved in closer. She peered in the window and watched Erika talk to the store's owner, an older woman with frizzy gray hair. The woman nodded her head and walked toward the back of the shop and through a door.

Erika had to be trying to sell the Gloria Canterbury doll, Kit was sure of it. Kit couldn't wait any longer. She pushed open the door and stormed up to Erika.

"I knew you did it!" Kit cried. "I just knew it! You stole the Gloria Canterbury doll!"

Erika didn't move. She stared at Kit without saying a word.

"Well," said Kit. "Let's see it."

Without saying a word, Erika reached into the brown paper bag. She brought out something wrapped in white tissue paper.

"How could you do it?" Kit asked.

Erika still didn't speak. She unwrapped the tissue paper slowly. Inside it was a baby doll. It was made of china and dressed in a pink, frilly dress.

It wasn't the Gloria Canterbury doll. Kit couldn't believe it.

"Satisfied?" Erika asked. A smug smile spread across her face.

"Gosh," Kit said, her cheeks burning. "I'm, I'm really sorry, I thought that . . ."

"I know what you thought," Erika said.

"Boy, I feel so stupid."

"You should," Erika said. She bent down to pick up some of the tissue paper that had fallen to the floor. Just then Kit saw a flash of silver.

The four-leaf-clover necklace! Erika was wearing it!

"Hey, wait a minute! What's this?" Kit asked.

Kit reached out for the necklace, but Erika grabbed it and held the pendant in her fist.

"Can I see it?" Kit asked.

Erika sighed and let the pendant drop. Kit saw that it was a silver pendant with a green enamel four-leaf-clover on it.

"Have you had this all along?" Kit demanded.

Erika sighed and mumbled, "I found it a few days ago."

"Why didn't you tell someone?" Kit said.

Erika's shoulders slumped. "I was too embarrassed. I acted like such a fool, screaming and everything. When I found it behind my dresser at home I thought about calling your mom, but I just couldn't. So I was hoping that everyone would forget about it."

"You accused Randy of stealing it!" Kit said. She was so angry, her voice cracked.

"I know, I know, and I'm really sorry. I'll apologize to your mom tonight. I was being stupid. I know it now." Erika looked at Kit earnestly. "And I didn't take that doll. I would never take someone else's doll. I know how important they can be to people."

The shop owner came from the back room, carrying an address book. "OK, Erika, I have the name of the man who repairs this sort of doll . . . ."

She stopped and looked at Kit. "May I help you?"

"No," Kit said. "I was just leaving." She turned to Erika. "See you at rehearsal. And I hope you apologize to Randy if you ever see him again."

"I will," said Erika. She touched Kit's arm as she was leaving. "I really am sorry that I acted so badly."

"Yeah, well, we all act dumb sometimes, like I just did a few minutes ago," Kit said.

Kit walked home slowly, deep in thought. The whole incident with Erika explained why she had been acting so nice lately, but it still didn't shed any light on who took the doll. Erika was Kit's main suspect, but now she wasn't too sure.

Then again, Erika was an actress. She could act innocent easily enough.

Kit and Mooch took their time getting to rehearsal. She still felt like she needed more time to think about everything. There must be something she was forgetting.

Crossing the parking lot, Kit saw a note underneath the windshield wiper of Mom's truck. She coasted up and then stopped. The note was written in black marker. When Kit read it, she felt a rash of goose bumps pop out on her arms.

THE SHOW MUST <u>NOT</u> GO ON!

# Chapter 10

# A Visit to Mrs. Pierce

Erika arrived at rehearsal and pulled Mom aside. They spoke for a few minutes, then Mom gave Erika a big hug. Later, Mom announced that Erika's necklace had been found and didn't offer any further explanation. It was so typical of Mom to save Erika that way.

Throughout rehearsal, Kit thought about the note. Where had she heard that phrase before? By the time everyone was getting ready to go home, she had figured it all out. It had to be her. There was no one else who disliked Mom that much.

As soon as everyone left, Kit showed the note to Mom.

"Who could have written this?" Mom asked. "It's so . . . so . . ."

"Creepy?" asked Kit.

"Yes, creepy," Mom said.

"I have a feeling I know who did it," Kit said.

Kit told Mom all about Mrs. Pierce talking to herself in the basement. Mom listened intently, but shook her head.

"No, it couldn't be her," Mom said. "I've known her since we were little girls."

"Was she at rehearsal today?" Kit asked.

"Well, no," Mom said, frowning.

"And didn't she say the exact same thing herself just the other day? Something about how the show must not go on?"

"Well, yes, but that's a saying everyone knows," Mom argued.

"Mom, she's incredibly jealous of you. She wants this show to fail. She might have taken the doll, too."

"Oh no, Kit, I doubt that."

"Let's go pay her a visit," Kit said. "I bet we discover that the costumes are just fine. I don't believe that they were ruined for one second. Didn't you see the way her eye twitched? It was weird."

Mom looked as though her thoughts were far, far away. "Her eye did twitch a lot, didn't it?"

"Yes."

"Come on," Mom said, putting Kit's scooter into the back of her truck. "Her eye used to twitch all the time when she was little. It always meant that she was fibbing."

"What are we going to say to her?" Kit asked.

"I'll think of something," Mom said.

Minutes later they were pulling up in front of Mrs. Pierce's dark gray house.

Kit rolled down the window for Mooch.

"Stay," she said, but Mooch was already asleep.

Mom rang the doorbell, then glanced at Kit. "Let me speak to her, OK? Just be quiet for once."

Mrs. Pierce came to the door wearing a ratty brown robe.

"Oh, Leslie, I'm sorry. I didn't mean to wake you up," Mom said, checking her watch.

"I was about to take a bath," Mrs. Pierce said gruffly. "What do you want?"

"Can we come in?" Mom asked. Mom looked directly at Mrs. Pierce with her big brown eyes. Kit knew how hard it was to say no to Mom. She would just keep at it until finally you said yes, so it was no use fighting it.

Mrs. Pierce paused, then opened the door wider and let them in.

"I think we need to talk," Mom said.

Mrs. Pierce gathered her robe tightly around her. "What about?" she asked.

"Well, I feel terrible about the costumes and the argument we had," Mom began.

Kit slowly started inching away from them. She wanted to find those costumes.

"Where are you going?" Mrs. Pierce asked.

"The bathroom?" Kit asked. "Is it this way?" She pointed down a long hall off of the living room. Kit saw a staircase at the end of it.

"Up the staircase, at the end of the hall," Mrs. Pierce said.

Kit could hear them talking as she walked down the hall. Mom was saying something about how sorry she was for yelling at her in front of the cast. Mrs. Pierce mumbled something about how the play was going to be a disaster and that Mom should give it up. Kit guessed that Mrs. Pierce didn't know Mom all that well, even though they grew up together. Mom *never* gave up.

When Kit got to the end of the hall, she darted up the stairs.

She hadn't told Mom she was going to snoop around, but it seemed like the only way to find the costumes. Kit glanced into the first room off the staircase. It had gray-blue walls and heavy, dark furniture. It looked as though it must be Mrs. Pierce's bedroom. Next to it was another door leading into a cramped beige bathroom. At the end of the hallway Kit saw another door.

Kit tiptoed down the hall. The door was just slightly open, so she squinted into the gloomy room. She could barely make out shapes in the dark. Then, at the far corner of the room, Kit clearly saw Alice's pale blue dress and the other characters' costumes. They didn't look ruined, the way Mrs. Pierce said they were.

She jumped when she heard approaching footsteps.

"What are you doing up here?" Mrs. Pierce demanded.

Kit inhaled sharply.

"Get downstairs!" Mrs. Pierce cried as she approached Kit.

Kit looked up at Mrs. Pierce's face. Her cheeks were streaked with red. A vein throbbed in her forehead.

"Mrs. Pierce, these costumes are fine. Why did you say they were ruined?"

"What are you doing snooping around my house?" Mrs. Pierce shouted.

Mom appeared next to her. "Leslie, what's this all about?" Mom asked.

Mrs. Pierce bowed her head and walked downstairs. She didn't seem angry any longer. Kit climbed down the stairs and Mom followed right behind her. All three of them wound up in the living room. Mrs. Pierce motioned for them to sit down.

Mrs. Pierce sighed and looked out the window. "I know you'll think I'm horrible," she said. "And I guess I am."

"We won't think you're horrible," Mom said softly. Kit wasn't so sure.

"Just wait. You might," Mrs. Pierce said, a strange grin on her face. "The costumes were never ruined. They've been here all along." She faced Mom, and Kit saw that the angry flush in her cheeks had appeared again. "But I'm just so tired of you getting all the good things in life, while I sit here and get nothing!" She flopped down on a chair opposite them.

"Did you write that note?" Mom asked.

Mrs. Pierce nodded, her eyes glued to the floor.

Mom breathed in, then asked, "And the doll? Did you take that, too?"

Mrs. Pierce looked directly into Mom's eyes and shook her head. "No. No way," she said. "You have to believe me about that. I may be jealous, but I'm not a criminal." She stood up and started pacing back and forth.

"It's just that I've always been jealous of you, Pamela, ever since we were little girls. You always got the good parts. Remember when you got that part in that Broadway play? You even got a great daughter," she said, looking at Kit. "And now, years later, I'm still feeling angry at you, I guess. I wanted . . ." She looked down at her hands. "I wanted you to fail at something. I figured if there were no costumes, then the play couldn't go on. For once, I would have won."

"But, Leslie," Mom said, getting up from the sofa, "I've always been jealous of you!"

Mrs. Pierce stared at her. "What? Me?"

"Yes!" Mom said, looking right back at her. "You are so creative! Why, I could never sew the kinds of things you sew. I can't even sew on a button! Many, many times I've wished I had your artistic talent. I am totally hopeless when it comes to anything like that, and you've always been terrific. I remember being so impressed with that poster you did for our senior class play."

"Really?" Mrs. Pierce asked. Something about the way she asked reminded Kit of a little girl. A shy little girl.

Mom reached down and gave Mrs. Pierce a big hug. Kit saw a glimmer of tears in Mrs. Pierce's eyes.

Mrs. Pierce wiped her eyes. "Well, I guess I'll bring those costumes back," she said. "I suppose sewing really is what I do best."

"Wonderful!" Mom said. "And we'll make sure your name is in big letters in the program!" Mom sat back down again, suddenly deflated. "That is, if there *is* a play."

"What do you mean?" Mrs. Pierce asked.

"Well," Mom began, "so many strange things have been going on, and the doll is still missing, and . . ."

Mrs. Pierce stood up. "Pamela," she said. "The show must go on! You said so yourself! What have the police said about the doll?"

"Oh, they say they're working on it, but I wonder," Mom said.

"Who do you think did it?" Kit asked.

Mrs. Pierce squinted. "I don't know," she said finally. "But I think it's someone who needs money. Very badly."

Kit and Mom exchanged glances. The only person who probably really needed money was Randy, and he was still missing.

Kit had to find him.

# Chapter 11

# The Search Is On

Kit e-mailed Spencer that night when she got home, telling him all about what had happened at Mrs. Pierce's and about her plan to find Randy. The next morning, after breakfast, she checked her e-mail for his response. Sure enough, his e-mail was waiting for her.

Dear Nancy Drew,

OK, we've eliminated (sort of) two suspects: Erika and Mrs. Pierce. That is, if we believe them. But I trust you on that one. Seems like you're a good judge of character. You're friends with me, aren't you? :-)

Randy is our last suspect. He was the only other person offstage when the crime happened, right? Or was there someone else? Think.

Anyway, you've gotta find him. Think of that $1,000! Which of course you'll split with me.

See ya—
Spencer

Kit thought about the e-mail all morning. Was

someone else offstage at the time? She pictured all the cast members—yep, they were all there, except for Erika.

Mom was buzzing around town doing errands, so Kit had to dig through her address book for Randy's address. What was his last name? Stemple? Stimple? Wait, it was Stickle. Randy Stickle. Kit practically cried out when she found his address. She especially relieved to see that he didn't live far. Kit's plan was to wait outside his apartment building. She was bound to see him go in or out.

Mooch waited for her at the front door. She hitched him to his leash, put on her protective gear, and took off on her scooter. The whole way there Kit thought about Spencer's e-mail. What was it that was bothering her about it? Within minutes she was in front of Randy's apartment building.

A woman with a long brown braid crouched in the small yard out front, tending to the marigolds. She stood up and wiped her brow.

"May I help you?" she asked.

"Have you seen Randy Stickle today?" Kit asked, stepping off her scooter. Mooch plopped down on the ground, exhausted.

The woman snorted. "As a matter of fact, no. He said he'd help me paint the front hall, but I haven't seen him in days. I'm not even sure he's living in his apartment anymore. The police came by looking for him, poor guy. I told them that I hadn't seen him, or *smelled* him, in days."

Kit wrinkled her nose. "*Smelled* him?"

The woman laughed. "Oh, I don't mean that he smells bad or anything. It's just that he has a serious thing for popcorn. I've never seen anything like it. He must make popcorn every day, sometimes twice a day. But I haven't smelled popcorn in days, so I figure he must not be there."

Popcorn! Kit thanked the woman and hopped back on her scooter.

"Better keep up, Mooch!" she cried, as the bulldog panted beside her.

Kit arrived home minutes later.

"Mom?" she called.

"I'm in the living room," Mom replied.

Kit stormed into the living room, startling Mom, who was on the sofa reading the paper.

"What's up?" Mom asked.

"I think I know where Randy is," Kit told her. She took a deep breath and went right into her story.

Mom listened closely. After Kit told her the whole story, Mom rose and got the keys to her truck.

"Come on," she said, "let's go see if you're right."

Without the stage crew and the actors, the theater was deadly quiet and dark. Looking around at the spooky theater, Kit wondered briefly if her hunch was wrong. Could someone really live here? If they were desperate enough, they could.

When Mom and Kit reached the top of the basement stairs, Kit put her finger to her lips. In the truck, she had told Mom that she thought it would be easier if she did all the talking at first. Randy might be too embarrassed to talk to Mom after everything she did for him.

Kit flicked on the light. Was that scurrying footsteps she heard?

"Hello?" Kit said, her voice wobbling. "Randy, are you there?"

Kit thought back to the time she smelled popcorn and mentally retraced her steps. She had been in her mom's office. Then she had walked down the hall to the stairs that went up to the stage. But before she had gotten there, she smelled the popcorn. It had been coming from the end of a long hallway to her right.

Kit found that hallway again and started to walk down it with Mom right behind her.

"Randy, it's Kit Conroy, Pamela Conroy's daughter. Can we talk, please? I don't think you took that doll. I really don't."

The quiet in the basement was intense. It was as if the basement itself was listening to her every word. She took a few more steps down the hall.

"Please, Randy, talk to me. I want to help you. I know you didn't do it."

More silence. Kit was about to go back when a voice from the end of the hall said, "Why don't you think I did it?"

Kit gasped. It was Randy! Her suspicions were correct! He had been hiding out in the theater this whole time!

Kit glanced over at Mom. She seemed just as excited as Kit.

Kit cleared her throat. "Because I don't think any guy would steal a dumb doll. It would just be too embarrassing if anyone found out."

The next sound that Kit heard surprised her. It was the sound of laughter. Finally, Randy emerged from the room at the end of the hall.

"That's pretty funny," he said, smiling. He stopped walking toward her as soon as he saw Mom. "Oh, you're here, too," he said, looking down.

"It's OK, Randy," Mom said, smiling. "I'm not upset with you."

Randy looked up at them both. "How did you know that I was down here?"

"Your landlady said you ate a lot of popcorn. That one time when I was down here with my mom I smelled popcorn." Kit frowned, thinking back on that night. "Hey, were you the one who turned off the lights that night?"

Randy looked down at the floor again. "Yeah," he said. "You were just about to discover my hiding place. I couldn't let that happen."

Kit crossed her arms and scowled. "You scared the daylights out of me! And Mom!"

"Sorry," Randy said. "I guess I was scared I'd be discovered."

"Are you the one who's been taking all the props, too?" Mom asked.

He nodded. "I've been using lamps and blankets and stuff to make myself more comfortable down here. And I found an old microwave, too, which was a real score since I could make popcorn. But I was going to give everything back. I really was."

He looked at them pleadingly. Kit bit her lip. She believed him. But she would have to convince everyone else, too. How?

"So you've been living here?" she asked.

"It's the only place I feel safe," he said. "There's a bathroom and everything. I'd sneak out every once in a while to buy popcorn or candy bars or something. It was perfect, until now," Randy explained.

"What were you going to do, keep living here until the end of time?" Kit asked.

Randy slumped against the wall. "I don't know," he said, shrugging. "I couldn't figure out what to do, so I thought I'd stay here until I got a plan. I know the whole cast thinks I did it. But I didn't do it! I didn't!"

"You should have told everyone that at the time," Mom said. "I know I would have believed you."

"You would have been the only one, that's for sure. I was in the wings when everyone was talking about who they thought did it. I heard what they said about me. I knew they all thought I did it."

"Well, we'll just have to convince them that you didn't do it," Kit said firmly.

Mom nodded. "Come on, Randy. I'll make you a nice home-cooked meal," she said.

Randy smiled at her. "I am getting a little tired of popcorn."

Kit glanced down at the end of the hallway and saw that Mom's office light was on.

"Hang on," Kit said. "I'm going to go turn off Mom's office light."

Kit hurried down the hall. Before she flicked off the light she saw the article in the *Clarion* again. It was posted on the bulletin board. She read the caption one more time. Something about it nagged at her. Then, suddenly, it all clicked together. Kit had the feeling she knew exactly who had taken the doll!

Kit was deep in thought for the entire ride home. Randy and Mom discussed how to get Randy out of this mess. Randy was right. No one would believe that he didn't take the doll. The only thing to do was to find out for sure who did.

When they got home, Randy and Mom went to the kitchen while Kit hurried upstairs to e-mail her suspicions to Spencer.

"I'll be down to help out in just a second," she called to them.

As soon as she was online, the Instant Message box clicked on.

**Segreti410:** Hey.
**StarGirl:** Are you always online, or what?

Before he had a chance to answer, Kit described the whole scene with Randy. She went on to tell Spencer of her suspicions about who the real thief was. After she typed the last sentence, she waited for his reply.

**Segreti410:** So what are you going to do now?

Mooch wandered into Kit's room. He plopped down on the floor and whined.

"Mooch, I don't have any treats for you," she said, scratching him behind his ear.

Just then a silly, crazy idea popped into her head. It was possibly the strangest idea she had ever had, but it just might work.

"Thanks, Mooch!" she cried. She typed her idea out for Spencer.

**Segreti410:** Hmmm, it just might work.

# Chapter 12

# A Doggone Crazy Plan

Kit explained her plan to Mom, who refused to go along with it at first. Kit reminded her that everyone thought that Randy stole the doll, and how important it was to find the real thief. That reasoning got through to Mom. She finally agreed to go along with the plan.

"I'll call a cast meeting," she said. "But I'll let you handle everything else. This had better work, Kit, or we'll be pretty embarrassed."

Kit rubbed Mooch's belly. "I hope it works, too."

The cast trickled into the theater, talking quietly amongst themselves. Erika looked worried. Mrs. Pierce looked as solemn as ever. Mrs. Greer trailed behind them. Randy came in with Mom, Kit, and Mooch.

The time had come to execute her plan. Despite her shaky hands, Kit dropped a dog treat into her suspect's pocket, just like she had done hundreds of times with Mom and Dad through the years. She crossed her fingers and hoped for the best.

"I hope you found out who did it," Mrs. Greer said, smiling at Kit.

Kit smiled back, her heart pounding like a marching band in her chest. What if her plan didn't work? Would the play get cancelled?

Once everyone gathered in front of the stage, Mom cleared her throat. "Kit and I have been talking about the theft of the doll, and, well, um, I'll let Kit explain the rest of this to you."

Kit stood before them, her knees as floppy as a scarecrow's. She wiped her sweaty palms on her jeans. Mooch woofed beside her.

"Hi, everyone. I know you guys are going to think this is crazy, but hear me out. You see, Mooch was in the lobby when the doll was taken. And at that same time, I think the thief dropped this." Kit brought the lipstick case out from her jean's pocket. She watched everyone's faces. Only one person looked startled at the sight of the lipstick case. Kit's hopes rose. It was a good thing Mom never got around to handing the lipstick case over to the police. She had been so busy with the play that she totally forgot.

"So, um, I think that Mooch knows who did it, and that if I let him sniff this lipstick case, he will then be able to sniff out who did it," Kit explained.

"That's ridiculous," said Sophie.

"Utterly insane," said Morrie.

"You're going to let a dog tell you who stole the doll?" asked Jeff.

That was just the kind of talk Kit was worried about. If she could only get them to go along with her bluff, then the real thief might do something to show his or her guilt. She *had* to make them believe that Mooch could actually find the suspect, or the whole thing would fail.

"Please," said Kit, "let's just see what happens. If Mooch doesn't do anything, then we'll know my theory is all wrong. But if he does, well, we might find the thief."

Kit inhaled sharply and unhooked Mooch's leash. She held the lipstick case up to Mooch's nose.

"OK, boy, who does this belong to, eh? Come on, boy," Kit said.

Mooch barely sniffed the case. Kit knew he could smell that treat in the suspect's pocket, though. And that he would mosey on up to the suspect, just as planned.

Mooch hesitated. Kit bit her lip, and said again, "Come on, Mooch, go on."

Mooch's big pink tongue hung out of his mouth.

He seemed confused, like he was wondering what this particular person was doing with his treat. Finally, after what seemed like decades, Mooch wandered up to Mrs. Greer and stood in front of her, whining.

A few people in the cast gasped.

Erika said, "Oh!"

"What?" Mrs. Greer cried. "This is ridiculous!"

"Is it, Mrs. Greer?" Kit asked, trying to keep her voice from shaking. "Is that your lipstick case?"

"I . . . I . . ." she stammered.

"You're the only other person who had a key to the glass case besides Mom," Kit said. "And you were there while almost everyone else was on stage, weren't you?"

"But, but . . ." Mrs. Greer said, her face pale, her eyes bulging with fear.

"You offered that reward as a way to throw us off the trail," Kit continued, "so that we would never suspect it was you. The only question is *why?*"

Mrs. Greer reached over to a seat and grabbed it, as if she were trying to hold herself up.

"Why, Mrs. Greer? Why did you do it?" Kit asked quietly.

Kit held her breath, waiting. Finally, Mrs. Greer sighed heavily and flopped down in the seat.

Mrs. Greer looked down at Mooch and shook her

head. "That doll should have been mine," she said, her eyes fixed to the floor. "I was Gloria Canterbury's only living relative. And yet she didn't give me a thing! Not one single thing! She was a cruel and selfish woman."

The theater was silent as everyone waited for her to continue. She looked off to the side, lost in thought.

"I've been in serious debt for some time now. I thought . . ." she paused. "I thought that by selling the doll I could get out of that debt forever. I am so very tired of being broke," Mrs. Greer said sadly.

Mom walked over to Mrs. Greer and sat down beside her.

"I've been feeling very guilty these past few days," Mrs. Greer said. "This morning when you called, I had already decided to return the doll anonymously. I am so embarrassed by all of this."

A tear rolled down her pale cheek. Mom reached over and squeezed her hand. Mrs. Greer looked at her gratefully.

"As far as I'm concerned, the doll *was* returned anonymously," Mom said, standing up. She looked at the cast. "Right, everyone?"

"Right!"

"Woof!" cried Mooch.

To celebrate, Kit and Mom had a cheese pizza that

night from their favorite pizza restaurant.

"That was some risk you took there, bluffing with Mooch the way you did," Mom said.

"It worked, didn't it?" Kit asked.

"It sure did, but I was worried," Mom said. "And that was so clever the way you guessed that the lipstick case was hers."

"Yeah, well, it suddenly dawned on me when I saw that article again in the *Clarion,* the one where it listed Mrs. Greer's first name as Gertrude. If her maiden name was Canterbury, then her initials would be 'G. C.', the same as the ones on the lipstick case."

"It never even occurred to me," Mom said.

"Who knows," Kit said, blowing on her pizza, "maybe I'll grow up to be a detective. But only if Mooch is my partner."

On the night of the performance, Spencer showed up wearing his baseball cap, as usual. Afterward he gave Kit a bouquet of daisies, and Dad presented her with a box of her favorite chocolates.

"After all that went on, I'm surprised it was such a success!" Kit told them, popping a chocolate-covered cherry into her mouth.

"Even Mrs. Greer seemed pleased," Mom added.

A woman wearing a fancy black suit shoved her way into the crowd and stood next to Mom.

"Kit, I'd like to introduce you to my old agent, Natalie Bloom," Mom said.

Kit could feel the blood rush to her cheeks. "Hi," she said meekly.

Natalie shook Kit's hand firmly. "You did a wonderful job, Kit. In fact, you were so good I was wondering if you'd like to try out for a television commercial that I'm casting right now."

Kit's eyes bugged out of her head. "You bet!" she cried.

"What's it for?" Mom asked.

"Well, it's for a toy company," Natalie said. "They're doing a commercial for a new line of dolls."

Kit's mouth dropped open. She looked at Mom.

"Dolls?" Mom asked.

"Yes," Natalie said, looking confused. "They're very fancy, expensive dolls. Would you be interested?"

Everyone was quiet for a few seconds. Spencer started cracking up. Then Dad. Finally all four of them were laughing so hard that tears were coming out of their eyes.

"Did I say something funny?" Natalie asked.

"Not really," Mom said as she slung her arm around Kit's shoulder. "It's just that we've had quite our fill of dolls lately."

"We sure have," Kit chimed in.